Off to SEE the SEA

words by **Nikki Grimes**

pictures by **Elizabeth Zunon**

sourcebooks
jabberwocky

For Corban Bates, whose boisterous
spirit can hardly be contained.
—NG

For Connor and Nolan!
—EZ

Text © 2021 by Nikki Grimes
Illustrations © 2021 by Elizabeth Zunon
Cover and internal design © 2021 by Sourcebooks

Sourcebooks and the colophon are registered trademarks of Sourcebooks

The characters and events portrayed in this book are fictitious or are used
fictitiously. Any similarity to real persons, living or dead, is purely coincidental
and not intended by the author.

The full color art was created using oil and acrylic paint with cut paper collage,
marker, and gel pen.

Published by Sourcebooks Jabberwocky, an imprint of Sourcebooks Kids
P.O. Box 4410, Naperville, Illinois 60567-4410
(630) 961-3900
sourcebookskids.com

Library of Congress Cataloging-in-Publication data is on file with the publisher.

Source of Production: Wing King Tong Paper Products Co. Ltd.,
Shenzhen, Guangdong Province, China
Date of Production: September 2020
Run Number: 5019344

Printed and bound in China.
WKT 10 9 8 7 6 5 4 3 2 1

"BATH TIME,"

I whisper in your ear.

You laugh
and then
DiSAPPEAR,

a master of
hide-and-seek.

"come," I coo.

"Bath time is full of magic!"

I switch on the faucet

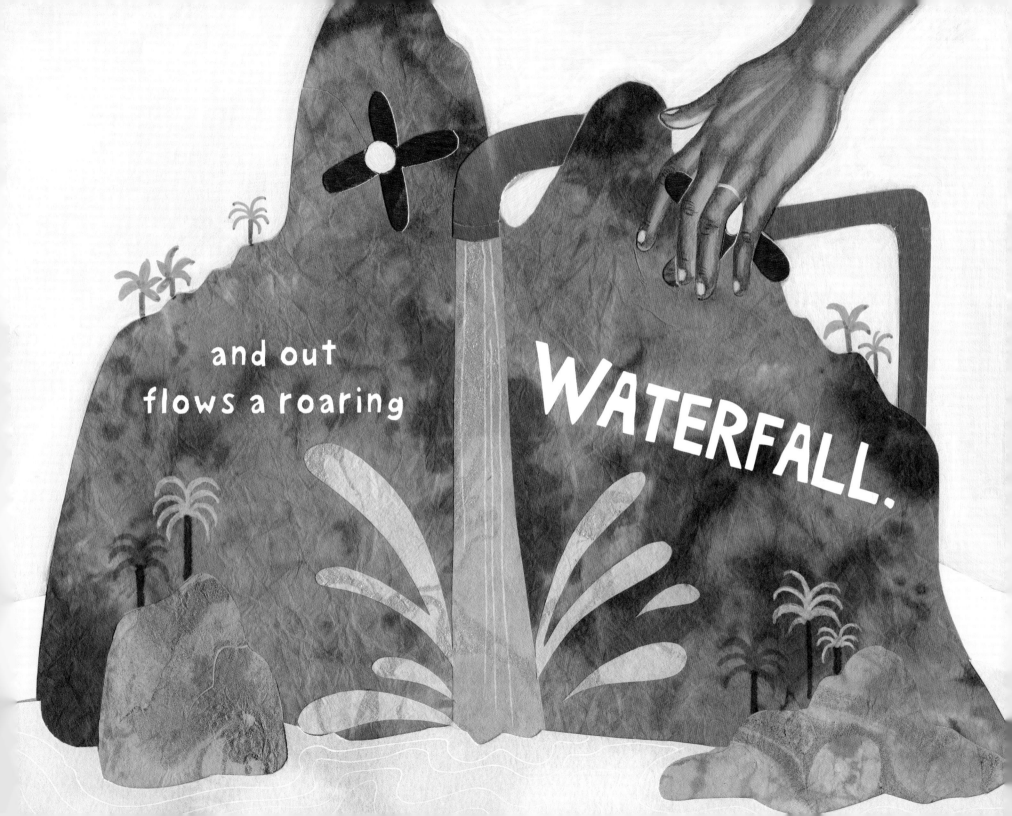

and out
flows a roaring

WATERFALL.

Up and up I lift you
till your toes leave the tile.
Then down, down you go,

slip-sliding
into a
SOFT-SCENTED
SEA.

"Now, was that so bad?" I ask.

You play pretend and **sniffle**.

"Oh my!" I say.

"MONSTERS straight ahead!

Watch out for the yellow rubber ducky!"

I warn, and you squeal.

Glistening soap BUBBLES sail into the air, shiny as mirrors,

carrying copies

of your smile.

You catch my eye,
then
SPLASH
over
and
over,

giggling as streams of water smack the DISTANT SHORE of the bathroom floor.

Before I can say,
"DON'T!"
you hold your nose

and

DiVE DEEP

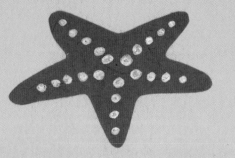

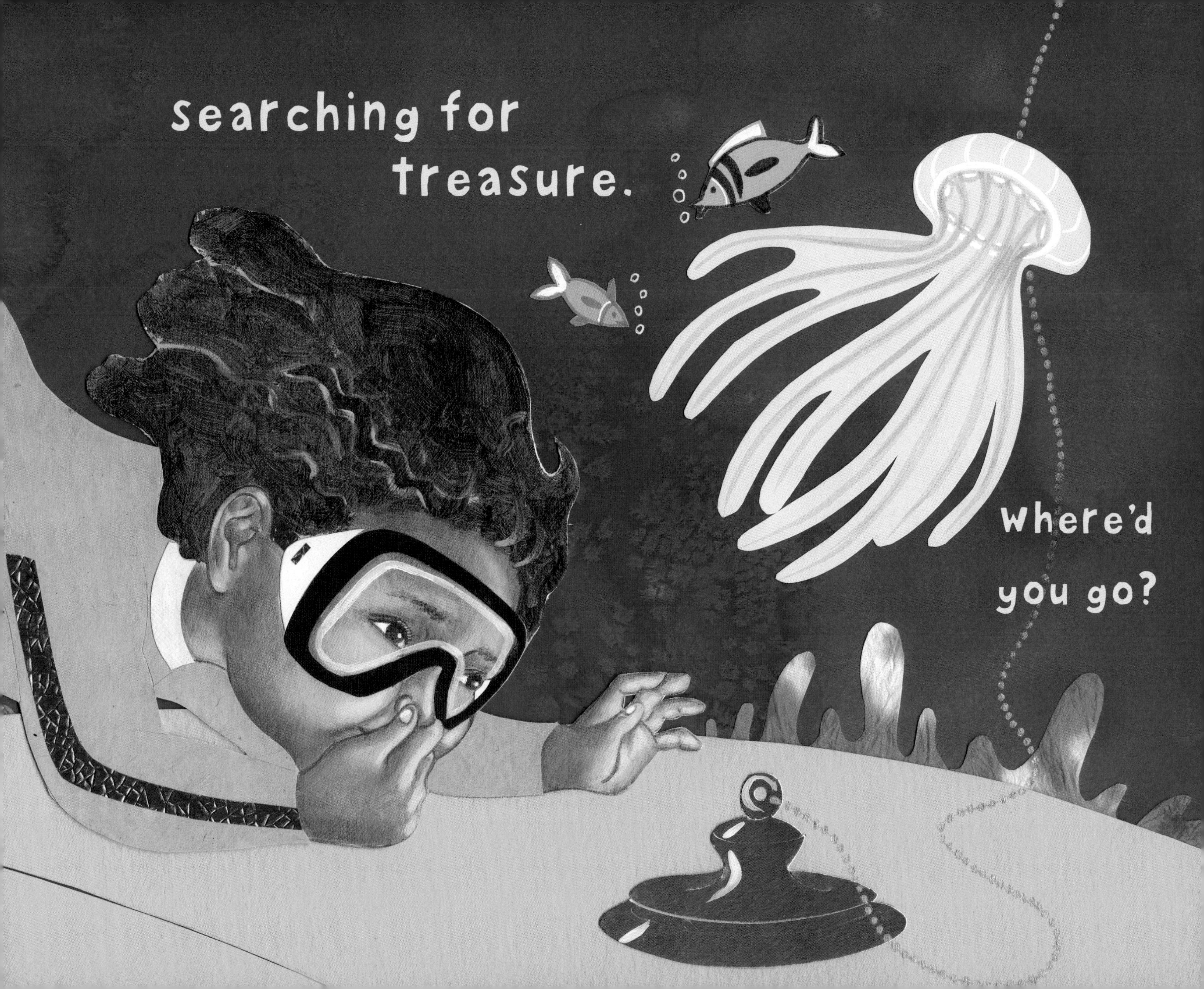

searching for treasure.

Where'd you go?

The twin **TUGBOATS**
your daddy gave you

CRASH
against the waves

your busy legs and feet
keep making.

I sneak shampoo
into your silky,
wet curls

while you flip the pages
of your FLOATING
bath-time book.

Faster than you can blink,
I sink my arm into
the cooling waters
of the
RAGING
SEA,

and pull
the
plug.

Together,

we watch the OCEAN

swirl

away.

TOWEL TIME, and you wiggle, making extra sure you're more slippery than an EEL.

"There now," I say

as your **toes**

touch

the tile

once

again.

You rub your eyes and **yawn**, ready to leave the **TEMPoRARY SEA** behind...

until tomorrow.

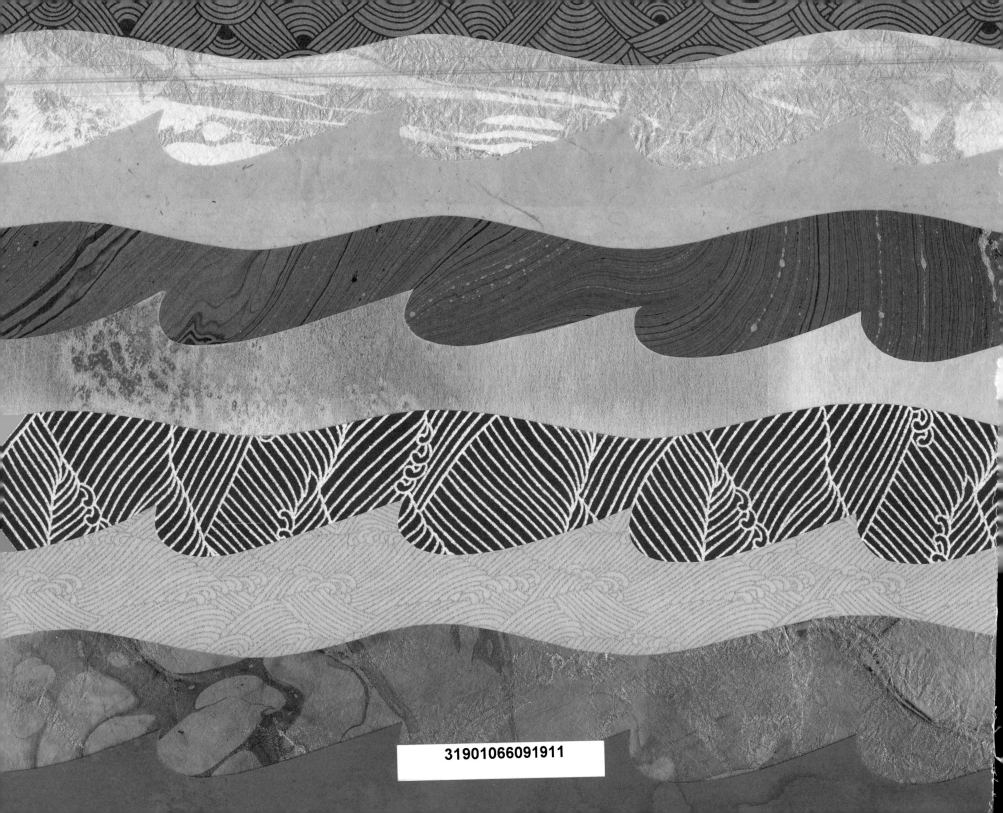